FEAR, WEAR & TEAR

ELEVEN BITTERSWEET SHORT STORIES

SHAWE RUCKUS

First published in Great Britain as a softback original in 2023

Editing, design, typesetting and publishing by UK Book Publishing

www.ukbookpublishing.com

ISBN: 978-1-915338-94-5

Cover photo by Ryoji Iwata on Unsplash

FEAR,
WEAR & TEAR

Contents

Pink Mail

It was one of those days when work gave me soul-ache.

I stepped out of the lift, reminiscing about my last holiday after a long session of brainstorming.

Or perhaps we should call it brain-snoring?

The lady at the reception stopped me.

'Mail for you; came in today.'

I looked at her hand, and she held out a pink envelope. The kind you could get at Paperchase three for the price of two. Or was it three for four?

I looked at the pink envelope again. It was a shade slightly darker than the Pink Panther. On it was hurried handwriting with my name only.

I took the envelope.

'You have a nice weekend then.'

I bid her goodbye, and she did likewise.

If curiosity killed the cat, what would bring about my demise?

Weighing the pink envelope in my hand, I thought.

A few weeks ago, while daydreaming at a junction near Tottenham Court Road, I saw a lamppost. On it was a small sticker ad, one of its corners hidden under a call girl's contact details.

One sentence on the ad caught my attention. *'Do you dare to put your name down here?'* it challenged.

A finger with a pink nail pointed to a blank line below.

Without thinking too much, I took out my pen and obliged.

I looked at the pink envelope again, tore it from the edges, and peeked inside.

A sheet of gloss paper.

It was a ticket to a button exhibition.

How interesting...

I went to the exhibition, learnt a few things about buttons that I could brag about during happy hours, but found no appropriate occasion to do so.

That was three months ago.

A second pink envelope came, then a third, then a fourth one.

They brought me to Ascot...a secret film screening... and a specific, exotic plant in Kew Gardens.

No quotes or claims for fees ever accompanied those pink envelopes.

Pink mail...

Was it a modern, urban version of blackmail?

Surely, no one would go through all this hassle to conspire against me?

I thought about it often on my way to work on the Bakerloo line.

I once read a story about a man who received mysterious calls at midnight from someone who claimed she had psychic powers and could predict the results of horse races.

The man had his doubts but soon ditched them after he won a dozen races. He bet high and won large.

His gains continued for a while, then, one day, he lost everything.

It turned out that the so-called 'psychic' made tons of calls and told all the receivers different results, and repeated the process...

Was I falling for such a trick as well?

Two more pink envelopes came.

One day, I woke up, brushed my teeth, had my toast with nothing on it, had a cup of coffee with everything extra, and decided that I had had enough.

I stopped at the reception and inquired about the person who had delivered the previous pink envelopes.

The lady at the reception told me it was 'someone from Deliveroo'.

There was no pattern to the dates on which I received the pink envelopes.

And my meetings always kept me away from the reception area in the lobby.

One day, when I was in the middle of a presentation, I looked out and caught a glimpse of a Deliveroo rider leaving the opposite building in a drizzle.

I made up my mind, went to the nearest Ryman's during my lunch break, and bought some envelopes.

I scribbled a note, put it in an envelope, sealed it, and handed it to the receptionist, who kindly agreed to give it to anyone who tried to deliver a pink envelope to me.

Then I was called away to fix a bug in the app we had just rolled out.

That was two weeks ago.

No more pink envelopes came. No more envelopes came.

One day, I retraced my steps to a particular lamppost near Tottenham Court Road and tried to locate the ad.

Like my faintest hope for some excitement, it had disappeared as well.

Last night, I prepared another envelope, this time typed out.

My resignation.

I packed my things and was ready to leave the premises when a Deliveroo rider came in and dropped off a small, pink envelope on the reception counter.

On it, my name.

I tore it open and found a card, with a meeting place and a time.

A restaurant that I had heard of but never been to before.

Now, I am standing in front of a florist, the latest pink envelope and its contents in my hand.

'How can I help?' The florist adjusted his apron and asked eagerly.

I thought for a while. 'What flowers would do for someone you have never met?'

Three and a Half White Roses

The first time I passed that flower shop, I almost bumped into a man holding a bunch of white roses.

It was one of my bad days.

I tumbled down the stairs at Euston after an eight-hour bus trip, lost my umbrella on the way, and was somehow angry at seeing those expensive baguettes and paninis flaunted on menus in all those grand cafes that might as well put out a sign reminding people to wear 'appropriate attire' if one wished to dine there.

The man was holding his roses as if he were holding a baby. I offered my apology quickly enough so he didn't say anything.

The flower shop had a wide selection. Some of them I knew, some I had never seen.

The white roses were particularly sweet and fresh. I stopped and asked for the price.

'How many, luv?' the florist asked.

'Well, perhaps...one?'

'That would be two quid.'

Two quid...

I did some fast mental calculations and decided that it was alright to have a little romantic expense on this special day.

I fished out my purse, found a two-pound coin, and exchanged it for a white rose.

Dami was already waiting at our rendezvous point, a place behind Somerset House where you could regard the Thames and its surrounding scenery.

He gave me a peck on the lips, and I gave him the white rose so he could put it in his lapel.

To do so, we had to break the stem, and a thorn stung my finger.

A drop of blood tainted his white shirt collar.

I could tell he was somewhat annoyed.

We walked a little way along the South Bank, had something to eat in Borough Market, and ended up back at his dorm room.

It was a small room but had an en suite toilet and shower.

There were books on his single bed. Old books smelling like yeast that he had borrowed from his university library.

He took off his jacket and put the white rose in a mug with coffee stains on its rim.

'You know, I did do my reading in reading week,' he told me.

We shared a kiss and kept our voices low, fearing his roommates might come and pound the door.

Afterwards, I took a quick shower and left to catch my bus.

The second time I stopped at the flower shop, I was already running late.

I had to change two trains and three lines to follow the best price recommendations made by my travelling app.

I would never trust it again.

I searched the purse in my bag in a frenzy, found a two-pound coin, and handed it to the florist.

'One white rose, please.'

He looked into his bucket of white roses, elegantly selected one, and handed it to me together with a shiny coin.

'A quid for you, my luv.'

I accepted the flower and the change.

I thought this might be a good omen.

Nothing pleased me more than saving money, perhaps except for earning money...and spending time with Dami.

This time, when we met, I noticed he had changed.

Like an apple with a worm at its core that never showed.

He started to use big words in his sentences. He would no longer say 'think', but always 'contemplated' on Rousseau and the 'social contract'. He also liked the word 'overarching' very much.

When he took the white rose from me somewhat unwillingly, he muttered something about the 'commodification of emotions' and how love was a 'social construct'.

When we lay in his bed, I showed him the new earrings my mother gave me for my birthday, and he told me stories about blood diamonds.

Before I left, he handed me a wrapped gift as a late birthday present.

I opened it on my train back home.

It was a book.

A book that his library no longer needed and he gave it to me for my birthday.

The third time we met, I was already grumpy because the white rose in my hand had cost me three pounds.

I could not stop myself but asked the florist, 'The first time I bought a white rose, it was two pounds, the next time, it was a single pound – why is it so expensive now?'

'Well...' he admitted reluctantly. 'I have to eat. Suppose I undercharge you this time. The ends won't meet.'

I paid my fare and exchanged it for a white rose.

Dami was late.

I checked my phone frantically, worried he might have run into trouble.

What if? What if?

A young guy sitting close by was arguing with someone over the phone.

'The world could do with one fewer economist or politician, but not without my writing. I write what I am good at and I am good at unrequited love. I have had tons of experiences at this venue.'

He hung up before the other party could respond.

Ten or so minutes passed before Dami finally arrived.

He was with another girl.

He introduced us. She was the treasurer of a society that he belonged to.

They had just attended a lecture on fair trade.

They talked about trade implications and the events at Chatham House for a while.

I had had enough of their small talk, and I intentionally broke the white rose and put it in Dami's lapel in a less-than-well-mannered manner.

The girl said goodbye and left us there.

'Why are you so fussy lately?' Dami rose and complained.

'Me being fussy? I was not the one who was late and didn't even bother to explain.'

'Keeping scores now, are we?' He took out the white rose and threw it on the table. 'I did not intend to take time out of my studies to engage in arguments with you!'

A drop of dew came out of the rose and mingled with the upside-down reflection of Tower Bridge on the glass table surface.

I was as mad as a boiling kettle.

'You treat me as if I were a book borrowed from your uni library. You flipped through a few pages only when you had to, and you speak to others as if you knew me by heart. You only complain about people failing, but you never see that they are also trying and struggling!'

He watched me, wide-eyed.

I left before he could organise any speeches that might hurt like a shard.

On my way back home, I passed the flower shop one last time.

The weather was black over Bill's mother's.

Dami used to say that a lot.

Well, before he began his studies in London.

The florist was preparing to close.

He noticed me, reached into the bucket with the white roses, and took out one with a broken stem.

He took out his specialist scissors and cut off the stem.

'You can take this one, luv. It's on me. Cheer up.'

I did just as he said.

I took half a white rose with me and left a piece of my heart there.

Life is Short

I **opened Zoom.**

It took a few seconds to connect.

Jamie looked beat, and he sounded like a flat tyre.

'You know,' I settled on my swivel chair, 'I'm afraid we're becoming zoombies.'

He laughed. 'Why such a grim outlook?' he retorted. 'I would say enjoy your staycation. It's all chaos outside now.'

I nodded.

He fell silent for a while. Or perhaps the connection was unstable.

'Alex, you remember Jacks, right? The apprentice who left last year?'

'Jacks, yeah, I know her. She left to go to university, right?'

He continued, and the kettle sang, so I excused myself and made a cup of tea.

By the time I returned, Jamie had moved on to complain about this online exam that he had to take.

'Have you heard that the Mexican place is out of business?' I changed the topic.

'How often we mused that we might find our better halves there...' he trailed off.

The Mexican restaurant had a huge mural and freshly made tacos. They also had a corner where you could put your business card into a jar, and find another diner who was interested in making new friends.

What Jamie didn't know was that I had never put my own card in.

We talked for a while, then he said, 'Well, Alex, you take care. I have to go and cram for my Certpay.'

'Take care, mate. And wash your hands diligently,' I half-joked.

'Roger that,' he said. 'And don't you drink like a fish.'

The call disconnected.

I closed my laptop and held my cup of tea.

My thoughts wandered like its remaining vapour.

I had first paid attention to Jacks on an autumn day.

That day, our shared office printer was out of order, and the external IT support staff was stuck in traffic somewhere in Kent.

My afternoon presentation was looming, there was no time to visit the closest printing shop, so I had to take the matter into my own hands.

I tried a few tricks, like turning the printer on and off; they failed.

Then I reloaded the paper, remembering that IT support always said it was better to put the smooth side down.

I fixed the printer miraculously, and only at the cost of a small cut on my index finger.

I sucked the wound, but it was deeper than I figured.

That was when I ran into Jacks in the corridor.

She had just returned from her lunch break.

She saw me and my bleeding finger, ran to her desk and took out a band-aid.

It had a happy Hello Kitty on it.

'Sorry, it's the only one I've got.' She smiled faintly.

'Cute kitten.' I thanked her and put the band-aid on.

'Life is short, and cats are cute.' She laughed. 'Family motto.'

Life carried on, and we didn't have that many interactions.

One winter day, she ran to my desk, her face distorted with worry.

'Alex, we got trouble at mill.'

One of our route planning apps had gone nuts and was misguiding users. One suggestion it made was that a cab trip from Waterloo Bridge to Oxford Circus would cost more than fifty pounds.

No one knew how it had happened, but most blamed the sudden departure of a previous product owner.

The destruction took no time while re-construction required us toddling around.

My team and I stayed late for many nights after that.

One night, I realised, it was only me and Jacks in the office.

'Jenny went to buy us coffee. We thought a little change in the beverage menu would do us good.'

I stood up, stretched my back, my arms, and my mind.

Then I noticed something in the building across the road – the offices were dark, but one glittering shape was moving.

Jacks saw it as well.

The shining figure changed colour as it roamed around and finally disappeared altogether.

I had often had reservations about those who were superstitious, but this was such a shocking phenomenon that I did not know how to explain it.

Jacks took out the pointer that she always used in presentations and pretended she was dowsing.

'I sense something.' She gave me a mysterious look. 'Do you? Perhaps I should message Jenny to pop into the Sainsbury's around the corner and buy us some garlic,' she joked.

'Bugger,' I said, 'if it were a Christmas spirit, I would like to ask him to help us debug this bloody app.'

She laughed and I laughed.

Then Jenny came back.

The app was fixed, and not by any supernatural assistance, but finally we had a lighter workload.

Days passed like clouds in the sky, then one evening in early February, I saw Jacks sitting in the waiting area in front of our reception; she looked unhappy.

'Jacks, anything giving you a headache?' I asked.

'Look.' She showed me her hand. There was a large brown button.

One of her coat buttons had fallen off. She was about to go to an important family reunion and had no way of fixing it on the spot.

'Lemme see.' I grabbed her coat and the button from her hand.

It was a little sweaty.

I took off my messenger bag and dug out a sewing kit, the type you could get in any good hotel room.

'I might just be able to help.' I opened the kit, pulled out the needle and a reasonable length of black thread. 'This should take less than a minute.'

'Alex! I didn't know you are so talented!' she cried out in surprise.

'Stop it; you'll make me blush. My mother always said that good boys should know how to sew on their shirt buttons.'

I fixed the problem and helped her into her coat.

'Good as new.' She examined the button.

'Off you go now.'

We waved goodbye and went our separate ways.

During my after-work commute that day, I felt happy and a little dizzy.

I held something warm in my heart to fend against that chilling, rainy winter night.

There was certainly something between us – or at least the potential of something.

Another day in March, we needed to persuade a switching client in Heathrow. Another teammate was supposed to join us, but called in sick.

We changed at Waterloo, and a man was busking.

He sang a merry melodic jazz tune.

We stood there for a while, enjoying the music.

'Must be one of John Pizzarelli's,' I mused.

'No,' Jacks smiled but said determinedly, 'Sinatra.'

'You sure?'

'As sure as the London Eye is in London.'

I gave her a look.

She laughed. 'Trust me. It's called "Tangerine".'

We boarded the tube with the last notes of the busker's singing.

I pulled back my wandering thoughts. I drank my almost cold tea, opened my laptop, and searched for Sinatra's "Tangerine".

I played the song once, then once more.

Jacks...

My eyes drifted to the time and date dial on my laptop.

April 1st.

April Fool's Day.

Perhaps the only time I made her unhappy was last year today.

That day, I had stepped into my office, and Jacks had followed in and announced: 'Alex, wish me a happy birthday!'

I laughed it off. 'Come on. We're too old for that.'

She looked annoyed. 'But it's my birthday today. Why don't you trust me? You, better than anyone, should know that I do not joke about these things.'

'Now. I do appreciate the effort.' I set down my bag. 'But we have a long day ahead.'

She was genuinely annoyed and left without a word.

Later that day, I learnt it was indeed her birthday.

Later that night, I did not go to her birthday celebration. Not because I was not invited, but I felt something had gone wrong between us.

A week later, Jacks informed me via an email that she would be leaving the office at the end of May to prepare for university.

She already had her BTECs, an unconditional offer from a Russell Group university in Central London, and she hoped to travel a little in Europe before her studies started.

We bid goodbye to each other – 'we' being the whole office.

Her desk was not empty for long, but a part within me was.

Last time I saw her, I was running some errands for my uncle that required a trip to the Strand.

I stopped at Temple Station and found my way around.

There I saw her, sitting in front of a Pret a Manger, rolling a cigarette.

I had wanted to say hi, but a boy of her age joined her and handed her a to-go cup along with a sandwich.

He picked up the cigarette she had just rolled, and I left, all of a sudden, in an imaginary hurry.

A week later, I was more than glad to accept my uncle's errands and re-instated myself in front of the coffee shop.

She was not there.

Of course, she was not there.

I lingered for a while, probably longer than necessary.

Life is short, yet life is no movie.

Only the brutalist building above heard my sigh.

April Fool's Day.

Another April Fool's Day.

Another Fool.

The same old fool.

I could still hear her voice. She said, 'Now, Alex, why the long face? Who stole your scone?'

I stood up, made another cup of tea, returned to my seat and thought for a long time.

I opened LinkedIn, found her profile page, and sent her a message:

Dear Jacqueline,

Happy Belated Birthday.

I am sorry.

Next time I checked, her profile was gone.

Money Crane

I got to the pub around half-past seven.

Old Sam leaned behind the counter, busying himself with wiping mugs.

It had been some time since the lockdown had lifted, yet you could still count the number of heads there with a single hand.

I ordered a pint of bitter and one for him as well.

'How you faring these days?'

'Couldn't be worse.'

We talked about football for a while and Sam commented, 'Least brought some good for your IT blokes. My son even got a bigger cheque, and all he does is muting and unmuting people in video meetings.'

I took some silent sips.

The pandemic might have been a boon for the online conferencing industry but was certainly less of a stimulant for the office equipment rental business for which I worked.

'Such a pity you got your hands tied with all this that won't sell.' He glanced at the beer crates that bore a name similar to the virus. Then he moved on to a distance craft brewing course he did when grounded.

I was about to retire for the night when someone entered.

A slender man, mid-forties, average build, settled down on the counter with a bulky manila envelope. He put away his jacket that smelled like the outside rain, wiped his hands with a wet tissue, removed his mask, and made his request with a heavy accent.

'Evening. May I have a Corona Extra?'

'Finally, someone with sense!' Sam gladly supplied a bottle.

'I work also in hospitality,' the man explained. 'And the outbreak has made me realise how much we are wasting.' He shifted in his stool and noticed my empty glass. 'Would you care for one as well?'

'And to what do I owe the pleasure?' I played at being formal.

'No, no, no. The pleasure is all mine.' He seemed confused for a second or two.

'Well.' I raised my glass. 'Won't do any harm.'

'Only more fun,' Sam joked.

I decided to stay a bit.

Loneliness has been a constant variable in my life, no matter the timing or location.

'So, what part of hospitality do you work in?' I asked after a few rounds.

'I am the manager of a *ryokan* in Japan.' He paused. 'In Izu.'

I scratched my head. 'Sorry, my Japanese is limited to printer brands.'

'Not at all. Our ryokan – or boarding house, if you prefer – is in the Izu Peninsula of Shizuoka Prefecture. You can see Fuji Mountain from our private *onsen*...baths. It's a traditional property, family-run for almost a century... very prestigious.' He recited a list of notable guests that the place had received. 'After the financial crisis, my hotel chain acquired it. They sent me to see through the transaction.'

'Must be difficult,' Sam noted. 'Going there and all.'

'Yes. Quite messy at the beginning.' The man gave a faint smile. 'The previous owners insisted that we keep all of their original staff. They even appointed me a teacher.' He laughed half-heartedly. 'I had to learn Japanese, and know when to kneel and bow, and at what angle.'

'With all their kneeling and bowing, no wonder it took ages to stop the Olympics!' Sam snapped.

'Mind if I ask what brought you to London?' I steered. 'Travelling must be a real pain in the arse now.'

He looked at me briefly, then looked away.

'I have family here, and my company filed for bankruptcy. They asked me to come and report my performance. Probably they didn't want to miss the cheap flights.'

'Looks like nothing is "too big to fail" anymore. Might they also consider places like us that are "too small to survive"?' Sam said bitterly. 'I don't know how long this old horse can drag on. Who knows what will happen when September comes?'

We sat there, each lost in our own thoughts.

Half an hour or so passed, then I drew out a tenner and got ready to leave.

'If there was one takeaway from my years in Japan,' the man said suddenly with a ragged voice, 'it was that when customers asked, we tried our best to deliver.'

I felt trapped in my seat and feared another long conversation.

'I reckon it's true, but you don't mean always?' Sam snorted. 'There are some beastly blokes, you know, making impossible demands all the time. Just the other night a guy asked if I could make his beer foam more "enticing". Bollocks! People are still dying and all he cared about was his beer foam!'

'Well...' the man hesitated, 'in Japan, they have this foam generator that gives you some fine bubbles.' He looked up at Sam, who seemed annoyed.

'And they have this word, *nominication*. It means good communication can only happen when people drink.'

'I wish we would do it more often. We should all get drunk and speak up.'

Sam relaxed somewhat.

'You are right,' the man reflected. 'Some guests did make difficult demands.' He cleared his throat. 'There was this gentleman who brought ten smartphones so we could help him with Pokémon Go, and this YouTuber who filled our public bath with gel balls that swelled up with water. We ended up having sewage rescue for two weeks. The balls clogged everywhere: lavabos, toilets, even our ponds.'

'Sounds like a bloody nasty business.'

The man smiled. 'Sí. Very nasty. He did pay for all the damage. But...' He paused. 'The most shocking demand we had was from this strange couple.'

Sam laughed. 'Now that you mention it, we get strange couples here all the time! Well, before the virus we did.'

'I'm in no position to comment on others' sexuality.' The man shifted nervously. 'Those things don't concern me a bit.'

I was tired yet intrigued by what he wanted to tell us.

'They were a couple, a man and a lady in their fifties. It was their behaviour that we found...odd.'

He sat up. 'They came in early January, after Japan's New Year holiday had ended. It was a smart decision because the rooms were much cheaper and the attractions less crowded.'

'Is it true that *geishas* sing and dance for you naked?' Sam inquired eagerly.

'Umm...not quite.' The man took another sip and ignored his question. 'By the time they arrived we were panicking. They sent a message requesting to be picked up from the train station, but the staff were so busy in the previous days that no one had noticed. So they took a taxi and when they came in they had this terrible face. It was like...'

A few touches of mellow laughter came from outside.

He frowned as if trying to recall.

'When the man signed the forms, I saw he was missing a little finger, and from the way he carried himself we guessed he belonged to the *yakuza* – the gangs.'

'Like the film *Outrage*? When you do a wrong deed you pay with a finger?'

Sam became interested.

'I haven't seen the film.' The man tensed a bit. 'We knew why they had requested a room with a private bath. It's quite common in Japan that if someone has tattoos, they can't use the public baths for reasons of propriety.'

'Got this one in Lima.' Sam rolled up his sleeve to show a figure similar to one of the Nazca lines. 'Will keep it in mind if I ever go to Japan.'

'That is a very cool tattoo,' the man resumed, somewhat in a hurry. 'The couple had no luggage, but the lady had a Boston bag. After they had checked in, they said they wanted to see the Omuro mountain, so we sent them out in a car with our chauffeur. When they got back, dinner was ready.'

He tilted his glass. 'One dish was Ise lobster *sashimi*. Our chef liked to decorate his plates, so he perfected that one with the lobster's head still moving, with dry ice and edible flowers, all the drama. When the dish was served, the lady broke out in cries. We were used to having vegan guests, but they would make their dietary requirements known beforehand. So I rushed in and asked if anything was wrong, and the man just sat there smoking.'

Someone came up to the counter, said goodbye to Sam, and left.

I excused myself, went to the loo, and washed my hands.

The man continued upon my return.

'Next morning, I found the lady in the lobby by the ice cream machine. We had it installed so guests could have free treats. She wanted one, but the slot got stuck. I helped her, then she saw the poster for instructions, and apologised for not reading it.'

'Well, printers jam less if you put the smooth side of the paper in, but no one pays attention to these details.'

I tried a smile.

'I saw them three times that morning. First time they were chasing a cat in our garden. Then I saw them by the pond with their hands in the water trying to touch the *koi* carp. Later they were staring at a *yuzu* tree. They were not happy, but they were not unhappy. They were... undisturbed, childish, even. But before lunch, the maids told me that their room was untouched.'

I listened attentively. 'Like they hadn't used it?'

'Yes. The shower was unused, the beds were still made, and the open-air bath had a layer of leaves and twigs on it.' The man shrugged. 'That was odd enough. I mean, you don't spend a pile of money on a room and then not use it, right? We began to speculate whether these two had been sent by our competitors, maybe as a prank, so they would complain about our service. It had happened before.'

'Had a few spiky ones in the old days too,' Sam commented.

'What we feared the most was bad reviews online,' the man said. 'So I decided to keep an eye on them. In the afternoon, the man went to browse our sword collection. We started arranging cultural workshops when the AirBnBs started to offer them. Then I saw her sitting in the lobby making *origami* paper cranes. But instead of paper she was using money – real notes.'

I looked down at my wrinkled tenner on the counter.

'She was using ten-thousand-yen notes, worth about seventy-pound sterling each. She saw me and told me not to worry, that they wouldn't be paying with the folded notes.'

'Blow me!' Sam said wryly. 'Some keep tigers as pets, some make art out of money... such good hobbies.'

The man continued. 'She had already made twenty or thirty of them, and she asked me for some green tea and biscuits. She liked the tea and told me about the Odoriko Super View train they took when coming. How cold it was on the platform, and *obasans*, middle-aged women chit-chatting on their return from New Year's trips. They reminded her of her relatives. I asked her about the mountain; she enjoyed the panorama of the bay on top. They saw someone trying to paraglide but they didn't manage because there was not enough wind. They also went to the nearby zoo and watched capybara relaxing in the hot springs. They reminded her of her child, who she had not seen for some time.'

A sudden clang startled us all.

A cursing was heard, and the streets went quiet again.

'That night, they skipped dinner, and we were busy receiving some foreign tourists. The next day, they had their breakfast, settled the bill, and left in a car. The man drove. That was a hectic day: one of our maids spilt a jug of soy sauce on the guest room's *tatami* flooring, then the tourists' son sprained his ankle, so we called a doctor, and the doctor called back saying he needed a car. We tried to locate the chauffeur and found him in... acts of romance with the second cook. The doctor finally came as we were preparing ice packs. It was then that a senior maid called me from the front desk. She was very discreet. I followed her into the room where the couple had stayed. They had used it by then...and we saw all these money cranes floating in the bath.'

'Oh! Do tell me Japanese money is waterproof!' Sam exclaimed.

'We tried to contact them and found out the number they had used to check in was unregistered. One staff member mentioned that we might just take it as a new way of getting tips, but in Japan tips are very uncommon. In the end we called the police.'

A cat meowed above us huskily.

'The police came, a team of them. They told us they wanted to inspect the room. At first, we thought maybe these two had something to do with the Ghosn case – the CEO who had escaped the country just beforehand. Later, I learnt from the ryokan's previous owners that the couple had got entangled in gang-related troubles. After they left, they had a car crash – their car hit the guardrail in Jogasaki and plunged into the sea. It was *shinju*; they did it to themselves.'

'Wasn't expecting this when you walked in tonight.'

Sam took out a scotch glass and filled it for himself. 'Makes a good bedtime story for my wife. She's into tragic love tales.'

'Quite a story,' I agreed.

'But you lost me for a bit – what shocking demand did they make?' Sam squinted. 'Did they leave any bodies in your place?'

The man sighed and squirmed. 'They certainly did not expect the pandemic.... Some weeks later, we got a returned parcel. Oh...' He rubbed his temples. 'I thought I had enough booze to speak up.'

'Go on,' I urged him. 'You don't have to tell us if you don't want to, or if it will get you into trouble.'

'We tried to repost the parcel, but by then Japan had suspended parts of the postal system because of the outbreak, so we couldn't post it. When they reopened, I was worried that it might never reach its destination, or that the recipient might...'

He sat up straight and looked up at me. 'You see, when customers ask, we try to deliver.' He smiled sadly. 'Even if for the last time.' He grabbed the manila envelope by his beer. 'I believe this is for you. From your mother.'

By the time I left the pub, the night had stretched like a leaked ink cartridge.

Silent Disco

I **sat down, and soft sand seeped in between my fingers.**

Laughter all around me.

In this Golden Week holiday, families joined together like a cast of hermit crabs on the beach.

A seagull wandered not far away.

Everything was so serene, yet the masks reminded us that not everything was as tranquil as it seemed.

A group of kite enthusiasts organised a small outing. They managed to launch several gigantic kites into the sky: one dragon, one character from Peking Opera, and one in the shape of a cherry.

A few others were lying on the sandy beach, not willing to fly.

I took out my phone: no messages, no calls.

Five past noon. I could stay a while.

A small crab crawled onto my left foot and escaped quickly when I moved my toes.

The sky was clear like a jellyfish, and the waves crashed softly.

A man was playing in the waves with his two daughters. Their shouting escaped their masks.

Aunt Emma had called last night, asking if I was alright, and when I would be going back.

'I cannot be certain. Tickets are hard to come by,' I told her.

'Oh! But I am sure if you reach out to the people at the Embassy...' She took a deep breath. 'Lennie, promise me that you will take good care of yourself.'

I promised.

She asked me to promise again, and I did.

She went on to narrate some of the terrible things she had heard were happening.

Later, I thanked her and asked her to take care.

A man walked past me and climbed up the white watching tower.

He didn't look like a lifeguard to me.

Perhaps he was just someone who wanted to have a better view after all these days of self-quarantining.

A few months ago, when Father called, I told him that everything in my region was under control.

'Now, don't tell me this, because how can you be so certain, Leonard?' he asked, rather impatiently.

'My school has moved all teaching online, and they have given me ten packs of masks, along with disinfectant, goggles, and gloves. There are community workers and volunteers in my neighbourhood, and they are responsible for checking the temperatures of all passers-by. Food is not a problem. We have drone delivery.'

He cut me off: 'Haven't you heard that millions of mobile phone users have vanished already? My boy, it would be best if you left at once. I insist that you leave at once.'

'I can't.' I paused and tried to explain. 'It would be unwise to travel now, given the circumstances, and I would need to travel from my city to the capital, or to Shanghai to connect to a direct flight to London.'

'Lennie, you should at least find yourself a teaching post in one of the metropolises.' He trailed off. 'I promised your mother that I would take good care of you. Come back, my boy, come back.'

My phone vibrated, a message from Zac.

I wiped the screen clear of sand and unlocked it.

Hi Leo,

I have good news, and I wanted to share it with you first.

Becky and I are engaged.

During these unsettling times, we have supported each other and have found that we were more than willing to become partners and companions for life.

We plan to get married officially as soon as the registration office reopens. I know this is a difficult time for you, but I would be most grateful if I could have the honour of having you as my best man. Please call me when your afternoon teaching session finishes. We can discuss the details from there.

I reread the message, did not reply but locked my phone.

Three years ago, I had started my first job as a junior auditor in a mid-tier accounting firm in the City.

The pay was adequate but not satisfactory given the long hours; other than that, there was nothing to complain about.

Father had been rather insistent then, always trying to set me up with a daughter of an old RAF friend, or a neighbour's niece.

Then, on my twenty-first birthday, after everyone had gone, I told Father 'girls are not my type' before leaving.

A few days later, he called me and told me that he had been so shocked that he had severe diarrhoea.

Or it could have been food poisoning. He wasn't sure.

'Leonard, I had always thought these things happened to people who lacked a male presence in their lives, like boys living with single mothers. Not that I have anything against...'

I told him that it had nothing to do with any such influence.

Then he asked me if anything, any accident or any abuse, had happened to me during my swimming years.

I reassured him that nothing of the sort had happened.

'On another note, Lennie, that night, I should probably have stopped you from having another cider as you were rather tipsy and you probably had a heavy head,' he decided.

I told him my lunch break was over, and he said we would talk later.

We met often and talked about the weather, football, new productions in the West End, even horses and hounds, but the 'talk' never materialised.

It was like an event that had been put on hold indefinitely.

We both knew we had to address the issue, but neither of us wanted to initiate the talk.

I felt awkward every day.

I was unable to bring myself to talk about Rooney or any other sportsman, because he would look weirdly at me, the way he would look at fundraising ads during Christmas.

That summer, I quit volunteering to teach swimming at the local club.

The final straw came one day when I was humming Jess Glynne's 'Hold My Hand' while mowing the lawn and Father shot me a glance I will never forget.

It was as if I was withholding a major conspiracy.

The very next second, I badly wanted an out.

At that time, work was giving me a big headache as well.

The life of an auditor was never enjoyable, and I had failed my CFA Level 3 exam again.

One night before the Christmas holiday, I was so depressed that when the whole office was gone, I put on my newly bought Christmas jumper that had lights on it, and my earphones, and I started to dance in the room for my own version of a silent disco.

I was just about to finish a song when the night security guard came in and I gave the poor lady a fright.

She told me that she had seen worse. You would never believe what crazy stuff traders did in their offices.

After the holiday, I met up with an old school mate. He had this service called 'City Escapade' for young professionals in the City wishing to try another career in a foreign country.

He told me that I could easily qualify as a maths teacher.

I considered the opportunity for a while and decided that I would go.

I hesitated a while before talking to Father about my decision.

Later, he told me if I were to go, he would lease out the house and move into a care home in Durham.

He had everything planned, up to the point of what school my children would attend.

The job application was made, the offer arrived, and the visa was granted.

A few months later, I relocated to a small coastal city in China with Seoul across the sea.

Father had always told me that he would visit me. But the visit was like the talk – ever pending.

The school I worked for was a newly built private school with a brochure advertising a faculty from fifteen different countries.

On my first day, the Head Principal told me, 'I understand that this is your first teaching job, Mr Jennings; do not be afraid of exercising authority. We have a very strict 'no phone' policy and a 'PSE' policy.'

I asked him what a 'PSE' policy was; he told me that it stood for 'Please Speak English'.

I took his words to heart, and during my very first lesson, I found a boy fumbling with his iPhone under his desk.

'Please turn it off.' I tried to exercise my newly granted authority.

I asked him to hand me the phone, and he reluctantly did so.

The school had a confusing combination of a British curriculum and a US school system where Checkpoints and GCSEs were taught alongside with homeroom teachers.

After class, I found Zachery Wright, the boy's homeroom teacher, and told him of his wrongdoing.

Zac, a feisty fellow, rose and shook my hand. 'Leonard, nice to meet you. Can I call you Leo?'

'I normally go by "Lennie",' I responded. 'But it's fine.'

'Right, Leo.' He thought for a second. 'Would you please show me?'

I frowned. 'I'm sorry. I don't quite get you.'

He laughed. 'Sorry. Could you show me the phone you confiscated from Kevin?'

I took out the phone from my teaching folder and handed it to him.

He took it, shook his head, and laughed once more. 'I knew he would do this.' He pressed the power button long enough, but it didn't turn on. 'Man, you have been fooled!'

Zac then told me it was not uncommon for pupils to acquire phone models from Taobao and hand them to teachers when caught using their phones.

He summoned Kevin. 'Up to old tricks again, huh?'

The boy murmured an apology, handed in his real phone, and was dismissed.

That weekend, I met up with Zac in a local pub.

It was also the pub that our Head Principal once favoured, but he hadn't frequented it after he met several students on the premises.

Zac introduced some of his friends to me, some colleagues he had in another school, and told me some episodes from his teaching life.

'So, for my birthday last year, the students decided to give me a birthday present. I was touched and thought how sweet they were! Then on my birthday, I had several new friend requests on WeChat, and I accepted them all in case they were parents. Then guess what? They gifted me a virtual mosquito, a virtual cat, and a virtual Avalokitesvara. So, I started getting all these messages and voice mails of the noises of a mosquito whining, and the meows of a cat and chanting. In the end, I had to delete them all. I tell you what, Leo, you better watch out because the kids will pull a prank on you whenever they find a chance. Their tricks are more than you can handle alone.'

He went on to say how much more he enjoyed his life now than previously as a primary teacher in a US public school.

'If there is one thing I like about WeChat,' he mused, 'is you can't know the reading status. Back in my days, my supervisor would bombard me with WhatsApp messages, and I had to reply when I read them because he would know when I read them. Do you like it here so far?'

I told him that I missed home, especially the chance to watch live football.

We moved our conversation to a nearby café.

The café had very decent sandwiches and the owner, Higgs, came from Aberdeen. He told me that his partner has recently started teaching in a nearby school, a notch higher than ours.

Higgs himself had been a teacher for a while, and he recounted an almost urban-legend-like story to us.

'There was a newcomer, a new teacher just like you, and he was an avid cycling fan. He brought with him, from his own country, a very high-end mountain bike that he guarded with multiple layers of protection. One day, he went to buy groceries at the local supermarket, but his bike was not allowed entry. He decided to lock his bike up to a nearby tree. When he finished shopping, he discovered the tree was gone.'

'Classic!' Zac exclaimed. 'You'll never get tired of the twist.'

'The tree was gone?' I shrugged. 'Luckily, I did not bring anything valuable.'

'Trust me, you did.' Zac looked me in the eye. 'You brought yourself, and you are certainly the most valuable thing in your own life.'

Higgs invited us to taste his new herbal tea menu. 'I heard the story from my predecessors. It was never verified.'

Zac declined the tea and asked for a cup of coffee instead.

I remembered he ordered an Irish coffee.

A lingering bitterness spread in my mouth, and suddenly, my mouth was as dry as cotton.

The surrounding peals of laughter once again filled my ears. I looked up, and more kites were up in the sky. One eggplant, one tomato, one apple...

A banner followed them.

Using my scant knowledge of Mandarin, I figured it was an advertisement encouraging people to buy more local produce.

I looked at my phone. I could stay a while longer. Or it might be better if I left and hid on one of the benches in the greenery not far from the shore.

Higgs' café remained closed, but he and his part-time assistant had been making hot beverages for the volunteers in the local neighbourhood.

Somewhere around mid-March, I baked a batch of chocolate muffins and offered them to the lady in charge of our neighbourhood.

She eyed me suspiciously and asked me what they were.

I told her they were for the volunteers. Becky translated for her, and they both laughed.

Becky giggled and told me that 'muffin' sounded like 'horse dung' in the regional dialect.

The community worker lady resembled Father in many ways: paid meticulous attention to detail, was never late to any meeting, and had everything planned out.

The first time we met – well, the first time I saw her – was a few days before the Chinese New Year.

One night, I heard a commotion outside my apartment door, and I peeked outside. Three community workers in their PPE stood in front of my neighbour's door; my landlord's as well.

The family had recently returned from a leisure trip to Japan. My landlord told me that the trip was wonderful except that his son had hurt his ankle.

Later, I asked my landlord about the commotion.

He explained that during their trip, he indulged his wife in a bit of shopping, and when they got to Osaka, they needed to rent four more large suitcases. I told him that I did not know there was an app specifically designed for that purpose. He smiled and said to me that it was the most convenient service. And once you were back in the country, people would come to your house to collect them.

So, he had the suitcases lined up on his balcony waiting for collection. It seemed that a neighbour across the building saw the suitcases and suspected that he was hiding people who had fled the city of Wuhan.

Thus, the community workers received an anonymous tip-off and were called to inspect the situation.

I told him that it must have been a rather inconvenient and frustrating experience.

He told me that he did not mind it at all. 'Mr Jennings,' he said, 'I don't care what people do as long as they don't harm me and my family's life chances, they don't harm others' life chances, and they don't harm their own life chances. In this difficult time, those with money have donated, those with time have volunteered, and those with resources have utilised them. Imagine if I did hide someone – would it not squander everyone's efforts?'

I did not know what to say.

Meanwhile, Father and Aunt Emma sent me many messages with what they thought was happening in Wuhan.

A few days later, my landlord knocked on my door.

I opened the door. He told me that he had just set up a mask-producing factory and would need some help with the process of achieving CE certification. I decided to call Higgs, whose partner had similar dealings.

Sometime later, my landlord showed me the masks his factory had produced and asked me if I would like to send some back home for family and friends, free of charge.

I thanked him and told him that the situation was not that severe back home, swallowing the unsaid 'compared with here'.

How quickly things have changed.

Once, Kevin had raised a question during an online session. He said, 'Teacher, you have had so many famous scientists and pioneers: you had Isaac Newton, you had Florence Nightingale, you had Rosalind Franklin, and you had Stephen Hawking. Why is that people still don't believe in science?'

I told him it was a complicated question.

A light breeze whirled some sand onto my face, and a few grains found their way to my eyes.

I stopped myself from rubbing my eyes, fearing my hands might be unclean.

A seagull flew among the kites and disappeared.

How different things are...

I thought.

Even the seagulls here were not that aggressive compared with the ones in London.

Back home I had seen one attacking and eating a pigeon alive.

Higgs' partner liked to watch birds. Perhaps I could send him a message later and ask why.

Higgs once told me that he and his partner got together because of a movie.

Was it a movie that they both liked? Was it a movie that they both hated?

Maybe I could ask next time.

I picked up my phone, unlocked it, and typed a quick reply to Zac.

Congratulations! I am very happy for you both.
And yes, I would love to be your best man.

I reviewed the message and remembered that Father had always said 'do not start your sentence with "And" as it is bad form'.

I hit 'send'.

I stood up, had another peek at the sky.

Somehow, the cherry and the tomato had become entangled, and the two kite runners were shouting at each other.

I turned my back and decided it was time to go.

And to let go.

A Purple Cat Got My Tongue

I climbed up the watching tower and stood still for a while.

Although it was late spring, the day was as cold as winter.

A dog barked somewhere, and I saw his owner chasing after him, leaving two trails of wet footsteps in the sand.

A few kites were up in the sky, and a few children were in the water.

A speaker nearby played a theme song from a hit movie.

All this reminded me of a day nearly two decades ago.

That day, my dad brought me to the outskirts of the factory he worked for and told me he had a surprise to show me.

'What is it, Dad? Is it a rare species of longicorn? Is it a trapped weasel?' I asked from the back seat of his bicycle.

'It's something you normally don't have a chance to see,' he said and turned. 'Just don't tell your mother or she'll scold me.'

'Fine.' I whistled a tune; a song called the 'The First Snow of 2002'.

'Say, is it true that the first snow of 2002 came a little later than usual?' I asked.

'Well. It certainly came earlier than usual round here.' He stopped the bicycle and patted the seat. 'Off you get now. We need to walk a bit.'

I followed his instructions and poked him in the rear.

'Listen,' he winced. 'You try to play doctor again, next time you catch a cold, I will ask the doctor to prescribe more syringes for you.'

'Whatever.'

I sucked on my milk candy.

We walked for a while and arrived at the scene of the surprise.

'Now, you see, young man, this is what happens when you don't listen to your parents. So, you should always stay away from fire, electricity, and water. After all, those who drown are mostly those who can swim. Or they believed they could. ' He pointed to the top of the electric fence on the factory wall.

There was a cat. A dead cat.

How realistic *Tom and Jerry* was, I first thought.

The cat was like a broken kite hanging between the branches of a tree. Spikes stood up from its fur, just like Tom when he was electrocuted in a story.

'This should teach you a lesson. Poor creature, his parents must be waiting for him to go home. I say we should bury him – what do you think?' Dad asked.

After that day, I could no longer speak.

Someone sneezed below, and I looked down.

A foreigner.

I remembered him. He was the one who made cakes for the community workers.

I caught him staring at his phone.

How enchanted people are with their phones these days!

I touched the whistle hanging from my neck.

Two years ago, one night, I was jogging along the pedestrian walk near the shoreline and saw a man pushing a baby cart, trying to cross the road.

He was so engrossed with his phone that he didn't notice a truck that was turning.

I blew my whistle like a referee mad at an offside soccer player and finally got his attention. He and the baby were saved; his phone was not.

A layer of mist arose from the sea, shrouding an island not far away.

Local folklore said that the island was where ancient Gods once lived.

My mother always said that 'saving a life is better than building a seven-tier pagoda'.

Ever since I had lost my ability to speak, she insisted that everything would be alright if we did enough good deeds.

Once, I wrote to her. 'Who is counting then?' I added, 'If saving a life is like building a seven-tier pagoda, then I must be a major estate developer in this imaginary, non-existent city of yours.'

She scowled. 'With this attitude of yours, we still have a long way to go.'

Fortunately, in my current line of work as a gardener, one does not need to say much. The trees and shrubs don't need comforting words. They have birds and insects singing for them.

A kite in the shape of a cherry came close enough with a strand of a cloud.

I looked down again.

Some crabs dug small holes in the wet sand and hid.

I was never afraid of heights.

In my final year of primary school, one day, the class bully stopped me on my way home. He said, 'I have figured out a way to make you to speak again. Do you know that rabbits squeak before they die? If you get scared enough, you might speak again.'

His proposal was enticing enough, and I was in no position to turn it down.

He brought me to the water tower not far from the village and told me to climb up.

'When you go up, and you get scared, you'll be able to talk again.'

I picked up a twig and wrote in the mud. 'Why don't you go up first?'

'This is about you, not me!'

I wrote again, breaking the twig, 'You're not scared, are you?'

'Of course not! How dare you dare me.' He thought for a while, took off his coat, and rolled up his sleeves. 'I will go up, and when I reach the top, you follow. If you don't, it means you are such a coward that even dogs laugh at your face.'

He climbed up.

Then, my cousin happened to pass by on his tractor. I went home with him and was just in time for *Tom and Jerry*.

That night, my cousin told my mother that he had decided to seek work in a coastal city.

How quickly people's plans change, I thought, or how quickly people have to accommodate new changes to their plans.

In the end, my cousin stayed in the village, and it was my mother who decided to move house.

Very few schools wanted me as a student, fearing my inability to speak might cause trouble. Many principals advised my mother to send me to a school catering for students with disabilities.

She said to one of them, 'A rich person has decided to keep his wealth in a safe. Then can you say he is poor? No, he just chose not to reveal his treasures.'

Perhaps the analogy was not flawed, except that I have no idea where or how to find my key to the safe.

Doctors said that psychological factors prevented me from speaking.

Only one principal agreed to give me a chance.

I enrolled in her school, and I cannot say that I have many happy memories from there.

My English teacher was a beast. He would scold me in front of the class, saying: 'Now, a shoehorn's place is in a shoe, a toilet brush's place is in a toilet, so where is your place?'

If it were not for my desk mate, a kind girl who always let me borrow her notes, I would have ended up in juvenile jail long ago for sure.

My desk mate was such a hardworking student that, after she graduated from university, she won a scholarship to study abroad.

Last year, she came back for a class reunion and told us she was getting married soon.

Many asked for the story of her exotic romance.

She laughed off the request. But when the majority of the class had gone, she told me.

As a gardener, it was not unusual to find drunk people pouring out their secrets to nearby tree holes. Once, I had to pry a man's fingers from breaking a newly planted sapling.

To a degree, I was glad that she told me instead of a tree.

Her story went like this:

While she was studying, she worked part-time in a restaurant. One day, an annoying customer tried to molest her. Luckily, another diner stopped the bastard. She wanted to thank the helper, but she did not know his name or contact details. Then her co-worker told her not to worry because she had the guy's business card. Her co-worker had also told her that her saviour had a passion for buttons.

We both laughed.

'Yes, buttons,' she continued. 'So I sent him a ticket for a button show. Then some other stuff.' She paused. 'I was not hoping for this to go anywhere, really, but my co-worker said that I should probably thank him in person. So, I sent him another note, asking him to join me at the restaurant.'

She paused again, lost in thoughts.

'When he showed up, my mind just shut down. Because...it was a completely different person; a stranger.' She reflected. 'Apparently, there was a misunderstanding somewhere, or it might be someone with the same name. You have no idea how often people's names coincide.'

She and the stranger talked, and talked for a bit longer, and found that they were no longer strangers.

After hearing the news, my mother cited some home-made statistics on how many of her colleagues' children were married and decided to set me up for some dates.

I messaged her: 'Please, Mother, it's not that you have an amazing track record in matchmaking.'

It was true. When she was young, she tried to matchmake two of her best friends.

It was half a success.

Her friends got married, but then divorced; what's more, one decided to become a Buddhist monk and the other a Buddhist nun.

'Maybe you would be better off if you let others consult about their career choices with you,' I joked.

She mumbled something before leaving the house to attend an event at the local community centre where elders scouted possible partners for their children.

My mother's plan had gone awry once more, but this time in a good way. Instead of finding me a spouse, she met someone herself.

My step-father had recently retired from the shipbuilding industry, and he enjoyed fishing.

One summer day, he came back home and did the dishes.

My mother had fractured her index finger while working in the textile industry as a young girl. For this reason, whenever we ate out, she would order by pointing at the menu with her middle finger, and caused some eyes to roll. When she met my step-father, he always insisted that he do the dishes and any washing to prevent 'humidity' from entering her bones.

After finishing the dishes, my step-father said to me, 'Today, when I was fishing, a young boy came to me on the pier. He showed me his phone. On it was a message asking if you could catch a small fish, cut a strip of meat off it to use as bait for a larger fish, throw the little fish back to the water, and it survive.' He paused. 'The boy also wrote on his phone that he could not hear, so I typed my answer on his phone. I told him that it was theoretically possible, but I had never tried it myself, and it must hurt for the small fish.' He trailed off and fixed his eyes on the TV.

The dog and his owner made a round trip on the beach. They chased a kite together.

I looked down again; the foreigner was still there, but no longer looking at his phone.

In my life so far, and especially in the days since I lost my ability to speak, I have learnt that when people talk, there are two types of messages they want to convey.

Sometimes, people want you to hear them out. Sometimes they want you to listen.

When people want to have someone to hear them out, it is no more than a gust of wind that sweeps sand one way then another; for example, with my former desk mate's story and my step-father's recounting. They wanted to find someone to speak to without causing much trouble and to let it out of their system.

However, there are times when people talk, and their words and sounds are like waves that deposit sand and cause emotions to sedimentate in your heart.

Sometimes, they do it unintentionally.

A few days ago, in the early morning, around four-thirty, I was just about to start my daily routine of checking saplings. I saw the foreigner sitting on a bench enclosed in a circle of Japanese pagoda trees, crying.

My English had always been bad, but I understood him.

He cried, 'Father...Father...'

I stood there for a while and took a less scenic route for my daily check.

Afterwards, I went home for breakfast. The TV news was showing the latest statistics for the COVID pandemic.

Mother sat and watched the news sternly. Ever since the New Year holiday, she had been charged with the task of contacting incomers in the neighbourhood and tracing their whereabouts.

One day, perhaps it was the Lantern Festival, she made about three hundred calls, confirming people's flight numbers, train numbers, and seat numbers.

My step-father carried a soup bowl and commented, 'It's still too early to let our guard down. Just last week, they found the virus on the outer packaging of some frozen shrimp imported from South America at the port. My buddies hurried to inspect everything again.'

Mother turned to us. 'You remember the foreigner? The one who lives in the high-rise across the street? The one who made cakes for the volunteers? I heard that his dad passed away in a nursing home in England.'

I excused myself and went to take a shower.

I looked down again. The dog had finally exhausted its owner, and the foreigner had left.

A change in wind brought some kites together, the players giving instructions on how to separate them.

The wind was biting, and I zipped up my jacket.

I often thought about the class bully.

That day, after I went home, he was stranded on top of that water tower. His parents thought that he had gone to play at his uncle's place in the nearby county. When the villagers found him, he was as stiff as a popsicle.

When the police inquired why I didn't say anything, I wrote in their notebook: 'because no one asked me, and because he said he was not scared. How could I know he had stayed up there all night?'

His throat was all swollen. They said he must have yelled until he collapsed.

How fragile life is.

After the incident, my mother decided to move house and gave me a whistle so I could draw people's attention whenever I needed to.

I touched my whistle once more, eyeing the surrounding area. Everything seemed to be in order.

I turned and was ready to leave.

But something caught my eye.

A black mass drifting in the waves.

Could it be seaweeds? Could it be someone's hair?

'Those who drown are mostly those who can swim. Or they believed they could.'

My dad's words rang in my head.

A hand reached out desperately, trying to beat the waves.

Someone was drowning.

I blew my whistle. Once, twice, many times.

Those on the beach seemed to be lost in their own stories. A few others were busying themselves with separating the kites.

How unfortunate; the speaker blasted out a song by an outdated idol group.

I blew my whistle, wishing it was a ship horn.

Someone sprinted into the water.

The foreigner.

A few others joined him, and they swam toward the drowning girl.

A kite in the shape of an eggplant flew across the open sky. Its owner no longer bothered to keep control.

The eggplant flew higher, its colour the same as my father's skin when he was electrocuted trying to retrieve the dead cat.

'Help! Help! Please...someone...help me...' I voiced, incoherently, repetitively.

Hot tears rolled down my throat.

News

He got up, coughed, and vomited.

Vivian came in. 'Darling, I insist on you having some rest.' She observed him by the washbasin gargling. 'You have worked all these years. I don't see why you can't let him...'

'It is not him.' He stood up. 'The thing is just some code.'

'But people love it! Because they all love John McLean.'

He wiped his face. 'An AI presenter could never be the same as me! It's got no emotions, cannot provide a timely joke or improvise! It's just a teleprompter with an artificial voice!'

He left without eating breakfast.

***

Ed was already there when he arrived at the studio.

'Morning, Jon. We'll have him on the show today.' Ed flipped some pages. 'Mate, you are a legend. Look at these, GAFT apps, a working contract with the RAF, even the London Underground wants you to mind people of their gaps!'

'Look, Ed,' he hampered his anger, 'I appreciate these, but people want the real me. And my voice.'

'Oh, Jon! We both know that you can't even pronounce "HMTQ" properly! And look at Sharina; she's been doing so well since the pilot run. I know it's been hard, but remember that your success does not stand without teamwork. And your family – Vivian mentioned that Maggie wants to...'

He didn't catch the rest.

***

He drove past streets and stopped at a red light.

A light breeze and birds' chirps came in through his window.

Some boys played not far away, mostly on their phones.

'Hey, McLean, tell me how your mother was.'

Its voice responded, and they all laughed uncontrollably.

He shut the window and put on the radio.

'Coming up next,' his ex-co-host announced, 'a dismembered human hand was found earlier this morning in Hyde Park. The police have...'

And its voice came in again.

The light turned.

He drove on, with full speed.

***

'British society in shock as John McLean confirmed dead in car crash.'

'Police investigate unidentified human remains at McLean crash site.'

'Dismembered hand found in Hyde Park linked to McLean case.'

'McLean AI removed nationally.'

'Homeless elder identified as McLean victim.'

'GAFT sue BTC over McLean case.'

'Family testify to McLean's lung cancer and severe mental instability.'

'Police confirmed McLean victim died of natural causes.'

'McLean case concluded as corpse abuse.'

'Exclusive: McLean's last words: "a replica shall never outlive its Master".'

Bowtie

After graduating from university, I went backpacking in Europe.

I had always thought of nature as an egalitarian form of entertainment. The rich have their way of appreciating nature, and the poor have our own means of paying tribute.

After all, who could say if a private viewing of the *Grainstacks At Giverny* is more cultural than watching the sunset on Velebit?

Money certainly does not account for all of the equation.

Given my meagre budget, I picked up various part-time jobs as I toured, played, and travelled along my route.

I made some friends; had a handful of fights as well.

By the time I arrived in Kyiv, I looked like a rat just escaped from its flooded hole.

I checked in to a hostel, made myself presentable, and went out for dinner. I had a few drinks, crawled back to bed, and when I woke up, I discovered that my luggage had disappeared together with my passport.

One might as well say that a leaking roof had met the unfortunate beginning of the rainy season.

I went to the embassy, communicated my problems, and the staff told me to wait for the re-issuance of my passport. I used their phone to call home, but was too ashamed to admit my stupidity and instead told my parents that all was well.

Later, I wasted my time in a local pub.

A couple of hours passed as I found solace in my drink, then a man approached me.

He asked me if I was alright.

I told him that I was a long way from alright.

We chatted for a while, and he asked me about my backpacking trip, which hiking route I had chosen in Slovakia, and what my plans were after my trip.

I told him that my original plan was to go back to my country and start working, but now, I needed to earn some money and try to finish the trip if I could.

He asked what my major was in university. I told him that I studied foreign languages – majored in English and minored in Russian.

He smiled and told me that he might have a perfect short-term job for me. Good pay, nice perks, and would allow me to make use of my language skills.

He said that his brother had a medical company that needed a translator who could help with foreign clients, mostly from the US.

He asked me if I would be interested, and like a drowning rat, I thanked him with a certain degree of desperation.

The next day, he showed me to his brother's company.

It was a surrogacy clinic.

***

The clinic had a modern ambience with several large Swiss cheese plants garnishing its corners.

A lady at the reception smiled at us. She introduced herself as Oksana. Her smile was as shining as Ronald McDonald's.

If a stranger were to pass this place, they might take it for a high-end dental clinic, with its Italian sofa, brightly coloured decor, and smiling staff.

We sat down and Eugene, the man's brother, handed me some leaflets about the clinic to read. He then reiterated his offer and the perks that came with the job.

Employees at the clinic enjoyed monthly passes to a local gym, had complimentary access to many local restaurants, and enjoyed special rates when renting apartments.

His list went on.

I was already having second thoughts and was about to decline his offer when a middle-aged woman entered the clinic.

She seemed self-conscious and asked in a low voice about the requirements of becoming a surrogate mother.

Oksana received her with her signature smile and told her that women needed to meet at least three conditions: to be over eighteen years old, to have had at least one child and to be mentally and physically fit for such a task.

The woman shot me a meaningful look before she continued. I realised she might have mistaken me for one of the clinic's clients.

She said that she would meet all the conditions. She had two children, and she was thinking of doing this for her daughter's tuition. She also didn't need her husband's consent as he had died in a riot two years ago. She then asked what the reward of such a service would be.

Oksana told her that the overall payment varied case by case and depended on if the couple needed an egg donation, but if one were to pass all the tests set by the clinic, the payment could be around 10,000 US dollars.

She added, if the woman was interested in becoming a surrogate mother, she could fill in the registration form and begin the tests.

The woman thought for a while and took up a ballpoint pen.

***

I sat there after the woman left, the clinic's leaflets crumpled in my hands.

My grandmother was widowed when she was thirty, and she paid for my mother's tuition by gluing matchboxes.

She once told me that, in the year of 1983, her village made a total of seventy million matchboxes, setting a new record at the time.

When my mother delivered a eulogy at her funeral, she sobbed that she had remembered her as 'a figure under a dim oil lamp, making matchboxes, her head bowing so low as if to touch the wood desk'.

I thought. How willing were parents to go through hardship just to see to their children's education?

Eugene made me a cup of coffee and flashed his smile at me.

He told me that the clinic adhered to the highest standards of professionalism in the industry and always took the best care of their 'gestational carriers'.

He also told me that the staff at the clinic had envisioned themselves as modern storks. They despised the wrongdoings at shabby local public hospitals. As if to further eliminate my hesitation, he gave me an operational handbook used by the clinic's staff. It detailed the very many procedures and processes that they carried out with the surrogate mothers, including daily balanced diet menus and exercise regimes.

He went on to address the legality of surrogacy in Ukraine, how we could work together to fulfil the wishes of people who wanted to be parents but who had problems conceiving.

He stressed that the clinic only helped heterosexual couples who had the material wellbeing to take care of children and who had real difficulties in conceiving. The clinic had also helped many local women, empowering them to improve their and their families' living conditions, and allowing them to realise their children's educational opportunities.

All in all, he said, again and again, it was a win-win situation.

I told him that I would need some time to make a decision, but I would consider the job.

On my way back, I passed a nursery where children were singing and playing.

I asked myself while waiting for the light at a junction, so far, you have helped to sell poor-quality souvenirs, sketchy travel plans, fake stamps, and cheap liquor. What would be the harm if you translated for a clinic whose services were needed for both parties involved?

I had my answer before the light changed.

***

By the time I received my new passport with a replacement Schengen visa and made enough money to continue my travels, I had already helped three couples to sign legal surrogacy contracts with the clinic.

On my last day, I shook hands with Eugene, thanked him for the opportunity, and told him I hoped the clinic and its operations would run smoothly.

As we left the office, Oksana had just consulted with a young girl who had expressed her wish of becoming a surrogate mother. The girl was getting married, and she hoped to save up for a full set of dental implants.

Later, the three of us had a small farewell celebration at a local restaurant.

Eugene asked me if I wanted to have some fun. I told him that I had an early start in the morning so I would pass.

We shook hands, hugged, and parted.

I walked to my accommodation in the crisp night air and saw someone sitting on a park bench under a lamp post.

The person was pregnant and seemed to be having a rest from her after-dinner walk.

I recognised her as the middle-aged woman who needed to pay for her daughter's tuition. Although we had met often at the clinic, we had never conversed.

I greeted her in Russian. She seemed surprised.

I asked her if everything was well and told her that today was my last day at the clinic.

She praised my Russian and said all was well except she had problems trying to refrain from drinking. She then asked me about my plans.

I told her I would travel for a bit then go back to my country and work.

She inquired what the prospects of living in my country were. I told her that life was comfortable if you had money, but if you were willing to work hard, then you would be better off.

I sat down beside her and tried to explain a joke that I once heard at a stand-up show: for someone who has average height, average looks, and average earnings, what's the point for me to not be mean?

She said that it was okay to be mean and sighed, 'but all men do is cheat and get drunk'.

I reminded her kindly that I happened to be in this group as well.

She laughed and commented that the daughter of one of her friends had married one of my fellow countrymen. The guy treated her so well she said she felt like a princess.

She mused that she might as well send her daughter to my country on her exchange term.

The night grew denser as we talked.

I helped her onto her feet and said that surrogacy was illegal in my country, but people do it illegally anyway. Hence some groups had been exerting pressure on the police to increase their efforts in tackling these issues.

She muttered, 'Maybe it is better that way.'

I didn't ask her what she meant.

***

We walked in the same direction, and I told her about some interesting episodes that I had had travelling during my university holidays.

For example, I told her how I misunderstood two words in Japanese, *suwaru'* and '*sawaru'*. One meant to sit down, the other to touch. And how I frantically panicked when a man at a restaurant told me to 'touch here please'.

I also told her why the Japanese company Toshiba is such a laughing-stock in South Korea.

She told me that there was a producer in Turkey called Arçelik that made wonderful and long-lasting products. She had known someone who became a surrogate mother, so she had enough money to buy their appliances.

She reflected that she was fortunate to be able to join this clinic where the practice was professional and well-executed. She had heard of a case where a clinic handed off the wrong baby to the parents, and after they found out, the baby ended up in a local orphanage.

She said she had asked her daughter to run some online searches for her; compared with clinics in Thailand and Cyprus, in Ukraine, the surrogate mothers' rights were legally protected and safeguarded.

We walked past a local farmers' market.

Oddly, watermelon was on sale.

I knocked on one, hearing that the fruit was ripe.

She asked me why I knocked. I told her that by listening for the sounds the watermelon made, you could see if it was ripe. A thump meant a ripe fruit.

She stood beside me, looking at the watermelons.

I told her that back home, we would eat watermelons and star fruits with a pinch of salt to make them taste sweeter.

She said she hoped her life would be the same: bitterness first, then sweetness.

I nodded, wishing her all the best.

A fruit vendor approached us. He asked us if we wanted to buy his fruits, and if not, not to linger.

We left.

As we moved through the food stalls, I stopped at the butcher's place and bought some beef.

We continued to walk and talk and finally parted at a crossroads.

'You are a great mother. I hope everything works out for you. And I hope your children benefit greatly from your devotion,' I told her, trying not to sound patronising. 'Please take this and add some nutrition,' I said as I handed her the beef.

She thanked me and wished me well.

Right before we parted, I noticed that her shoelaces were loose – something Eugene would call a 'production safety hazard'.

She tried to bend down but struggled.

'Let me help,' I offered.

She sported a pair of Adidas, courtesy of the clinic.

I made a double knot with a bowtie on each side. 'This way, it won't fall out.'

We said farewell to each other again, and one turned left and the other right.

***

Having completed my travels, I went back to my country and started my job hunt.

I did not feel the need to add the stint as 'consultant' in Kyiv to my updated CV, and in the end, I joined an e-commerce company.

After initial training and orientation, I went into procurement. Our department was responsible for sourcing all the best products from foreign countries.

The senior members of staff went to procure cosmetics from Japan, nutritional supplements from the US, and raincoats from the UK, while the newcomers were assigned less appealing places.

One friend went to procure fedora hats from Ecuador. Another went to Tanzania to buy sesame seeds. I was assigned to Ukraine to negotiate with the maker of a famous brand of biscuits.

I checked into the Hyatt and decided to have a stroll after dinner.

Nothing seemed to have changed, but when you feel secure, when you feel you have a sturdy roof that you can return to, you feel you have changed.

I had a drink at a local pub, the same one where Eugene's brother offered me a job.

I took my time to explore the area, and I walked back to my hotel shortly before midnight.

Two blocks away from my destination, I bumped into a woman.

She recognised me and smiled faintly.

I asked her how she had been.

She told me that the baby suffered from a rare case of nuchal cord, and she had a stillbirth.

She also said the clinic had allowed her a period of recovery, and they would help her to deliver another one as per the contract. If all went well, her next delivery date would be in July 2020, just in time for the Olympics.

We walked silently for a while.

She asked me where I was staying, and I told her.

Then she asked me if I'd like some company for the evening, and I said no.

She said she would walk me back to the hotel.

We stopped at a junction, and both of us noticed that her shoelaces were loose.

She was wearing the same pair of Adidas.

'Aha,' she commented lightheartedly, 'at least now I can tie my shoelaces.'

She bent down to tie them.

But I knew she was crying.

A Good Cry

I **came to the UK in 2014 at the age of nineteen.**

It was my first time travelling anywhere abroad, let alone by myself.

I got off the plane, found my luggage, felt relieved that nothing was stolen or amiss, and made my way to a pre-booked car.

The driver helped me with my bags, and we discussed many things on the way: the weather, football, politics, and what was new in town.

By the time we arrived at our destination, he had commented that I spoke excellent English and he had understood 'every single word of it'.

I was not sure whether to be glad or upset.

My allocated university accommodation was in Southwark. It had a name borrowed from an old James Bond film.

Because of a delay in the issuance of my CAS number, I only obtained my visa two weeks later into my course. I felt bad and sad that I had missed most of the welcome events.

I dragged my luggage and got into my room. It looked smaller than in the pictures.

I unpacked quickly and found my way to the common area. Being a weekday, no one was in there.

I had known earlier that I had three roommates sharing the same floor, whose information I had learnt by heart before boarding.

There was a British boy called Damian, a Chinese girl named Man (what a name!), and a Swiss girl called Carlisle.

Growing up in a large household, I understood too well the difficulties and necessities of avoiding conflicts. And as a child with many siblings, I had often credited myself with the ability to demand less attention.

By evening, my roommates had returned from their various lectures and seminars. After a brief round of introductions, I discovered that we had more in common than the fact that we attended the same university.

Damian and I supported Manchester City. Man and I shared a passion for cooking. Carlisle liked the same rapper as I did.

Other than that, all of our parents worked in the beverage industry.

My father made his living as a Coca-Cola distributor. Dami came from a town famous for cider, and his parents worked in the local brewery. Man's parents nurtured grapes for a large winery in China, hence her name, she explained; 'man' means 'vine' in Mandarin. Carlisle's father was on the WHO's Alcohol Policy Strategic Advisory Committee. She told us that her father was working on a special report on global alcohol consumption.

Dami was kind enough to show me around. There was a small café around the corner and a gym beside it. We went to a Sainsbury's and bought sandwiches. We ate as we walked. He asked me if I was interested in an event on Samuel Jackson at the Gresham College that he was attending later in the evening.

I said, why not.

Only by the time we arrived at the venue, I realised that he meant Samuel Johnson.

What a night.

***

I would say that the four of us made a good group.

At least no one stole from the refrigerator.

One course mate of mine had complained that he needed to put lockable boxes inside the fridge, so his food did not draw unwanted attention.

I had often wondered if aliens were real. University accommodation would be the most appropriate experimental field for extra-terrestrial beings to observe humans and obtain insights on how we live.

Although living under the same roof, our lives differed like planets in the solar systems.

Man had a friend who drove a Bentley, but she would always get back to her room before nine in the evening. Once, returning from a lecture, I bumped into her around the corner and caught her staring into the gym's window. Someone was exhausting himself with the battle ropes.

I asked her if she was going to join the gym, but she said that her parents had always told her to study hard so she could earn money doing mental work. She smiled and said, 'I have never used a gym. I suppose I don't want to spend my money earned from mental labour on physical work.'

Carlisle, the Swiss girl, would call home every Friday night. One time, I walked into the kitchen and overheard her talking on her phone. She chuckled to the other end and said, 'Nah, my horse riding is patchy but okay. I can sail very well, though.'

Dami came to study in London on a scholarship, and as a first-generation college student, he confessed to me that he had been under a lot of strain. His girlfriend would come and visit him sometimes.

I had met her once.

One day, I spent some time at the library working on a question set and went back to my room, feeling all shitty.

I saw Dami and his girlfriend in the corridor, and we said hi before the couple quickly escaped into their room.

It was reading week. I could vaguely recall that they were discussing a travel plan of some sort. I heard Dami tell the girl not to worry; that he would 'get off at Gateshead'.

I had never travelled by train in the UK.

Well, perhaps that was not entirely accurate. I did once use the train to visit a cousin at Warwick.

For someone who had never used an urban metro system, I found the London Underground a complete haze.

And you had no idea what strange people you could meet.

Once I saw a half-naked man with his lower-half apparel missing. Another time, a lady with a parrot on her shoulder. And a man who meowed all the time.

What a world.

***

Like many university students, I acquired a bike as my primary mode of transportation. I bought a folding bike, not knowing how many hands it had passed through, and brought it to a bike shop near my main campus for inspection.

The place had a broken light bulb that flashed like a firefly.

A man examined the bike and told me that what I needed was a 'jungle service'.

I was livid at this direct, racist comment.

So, I asked him, 'What do you mean by a "jungle service" sir!'

He looked shocked and responded that what I needed was a *general service*.

I apologised for my mishearing, and he told me it was all fine.

Before I left the store, he summoned one of his assistants and said to him, 'A general service for this young man and ain't it as dim as a TH lamp?'

I looked up, and the light bulb overhead was indeed very dim.

My nan had always said that when people make mistakes, they learn their lessons well.

I certainly learnt mine after crashing my bike onto the kerb for the second time in a week.

The first time I grazed my knees, and I had less luck on the second occasion, fracturing my right arm.

In my GP's waiting room, I met a man who had broken his leg in a traffic accident. Poor Martin, he cursed the driver while we waited for our appointments. The doctor prescribed him codeine, and Martin told me, 'Good luck with your studies, young lad, and don't you ever break a leg. It's too much pain and trouble.'

I thanked him for his kind words and told him to take care.

With my preferred mode of transportation out of the question, I walked to school every day.

On my way, I had discovered a garden that had been a mass burial ground for the poor for centuries. It was called 'Crossbones'.

I told the story of the garden to my nan over the phone, and she requested me to alter my route. She had always worried about my safety.

She said, 'My boy, who knows who or what might be lurking in the shadows?'

What a question!

***

After my bike accident, my roommates had been most helpful to my recovery.

Dami sometimes assisted me with the shower adjustments. Man often cooked more than she could eat and told me that it was a sin to waste food. Carlisle had offered me advice on how to recover faster.

Man told us that there was a saying in Chinese: 'good neighbours beat distant relatives'.

I was fortunate to have such good roommates. But there was also a saying in my country: 'a rented place is no comparison to a home'.

As Christmas neared, my earnestness to go home turned into worry.

One day, I got a call informing me that my nan had been hospitalised, and that her condition was concerning.

I told her that I could leave early. She persuaded me to stay.

She said she had lived a life with only a few regrets. And she was proud that she had left no debts.

The news of her passing away finally came on a Saturday evening.

Back home, after fights with elder siblings, I liked to cry while swimming – hot tears infusing with cold water, an all different sensation.

After all, who could distinguish tears from water?

And red eyes certainly went well with chlorine water.

I desperately hoped that the gym had a swimming pool. But it was too small to accommodate one.

I got into the shower with the water running, and started crying.

I cried for a while.

Then, I towelled myself off, took a few painkillers, and got into bed.

Before I drifted into sleep, I faintly heard sobbing down the corridor.

I was not sure if it was Dami, or Man, or Carlisle.

Perhaps happiness we could share, but sadness we could not.

***

My nan had a philosophy on crying.

She insisted that we all need a good cry sometimes.

She once told me, 'My boy. Do you know what you should do when you see someone crying? There are several tactics. The worst one is to ask them to stop crying, for it stops their natural way of expressing themselves. Crying is a way of detoxing. And have you ever heard of someone trying to tell another human not to sneeze? If they tried to stop from sneezing forcibly, their eyeballs could explode.'

She said that she had once witnessed such a happening when she was younger.

'A better way,' she said, 'is to sit with them. Saying nothing. Or leave them alone for a moment. Let them be and let them cry.'

Some years later, I read a story about a woman who heard another crying in a public toilet. She read a poem about crying to console the tear shedder.

I wished I could ask my nan on her opinion on this new tactic.

Life passed like cars on Waterloo Bridge. And shortly before Christmas vacation, Dami asked me if I had time that evening. My roommates thought it would be nice to have a night together before we went back home.

My mood had lifted since I had had a good cry.

'I've got the time if you've got the inclination.'

I borrowed a joke from my Engineering lecturer.

'Wicked! See you tonight.'

I started my day in the usual way: a morning lecture, some hours in the library, and a long-time mourning.

I got back to my dorm. The kitchen was dark, just like the first time I had walked in two months ago.

Suddenly, lights shined, and candles flickered. Dami held a small birthday cake with my name on it.

'Happy birthday to you...'

My roommates started to sing.

I had forgotten all about my birthday.

Unlike most families, my birthday was not celebrated often, and only my nan would remember it.

But I could no longer call her, I could no longer hear her stories, and I could no longer see her watering her plants back home.

The song finished. My three roommates stood there, waiting for me to speak.

'Thank you, guys.' I forced my voice to steady. 'I'm really touched.'

'Now make a wish,' Carlisle prompted.

I stepped in front of the cake. It had chocolate and berries, apricots and cherries.

Could you wish for something that would never come true? I wondered as I looked at the cake.

There was only so much pain we can withhold. The kind that codeine tablets won't treat.

My wish did not put off the candles. My tears did.

They reflected no gratitude and only sadness.

My roommates were surprised at this turn of events.

A few seconds later, I was surprised.

Dami put down the cake with shaky hands and started crying.

He walked to the sink, dipped his head in it, and his teardrops drummed on the metal.

Then Man started to sob, the same sobbing I had heard on the evening of my nan's passing.

Carlisle snuffled. Her tears flowed quietly, her mascara running.

We cried for minutes.

That night, I learnt that when you see people crying, the worst thing is to ask them to stop; a better way is to leave them alone, and the best way is to cry with them.

***

Dami washed his face and handed pieces of kitchen towel to us. We wiped our faces, and the girls retreated to their rooms to reapply their makeup.

Later, we shared the cake and talked about why we had cried as if we were discussing a seminar question.

I started with the cause of my sorrow. I told them that my nan was not my grandmother, but a helper we had had since my mother passed away. She had treated me even better than my grandmother. Now that she was gone, I did not even want to go back home.

Dami said he felt bad about going home too. He had broken things off with his girlfriend, but he would for sure see her during Christmas celebrations. He sighed, 'It's a small town.' He also said that he had tried very hard to make their long-distance relationship work. And for her birthday present, he had searched and searched and finally found a copy of *The Poems of Samuel Johnson* in an antique book shop near Waterloo Bridge.

I had been to that book shop. It had old Marvel comics that I bought for my younger sister.

Man told us that her parents were planning to visit her in London. But their visa application had been rejected, and they were placed on a ten-year visa ban. A letter accompanying the embassy's decision said that the staff were suspicious why these two farmers, who had never travelled aboard, had a very large sum of money in their bank accounts.

Man explained to us that although her parents had never travelled abroad, they had spent their time leading a thousand-acre vineyard. And she had found a reliable solicitor to try to overturn the ban.

Carlisle told us that she was under a lot of stress because she had decided to change course and had re-applied to Oxford. She had a demanding schedule balancing her current studies, mock interview, and test preparations. She added timidly that Man and I had been pronouncing her name the wrong way all along.

It was pronounced as 'Carl-aisle', not 'Car-lis-le'.

The two of us apologised.

I elbowed Dami and asked him why he didn't point it out to us. He responded that he was afraid that we'd be offended.

We talked for a little longer. Then someone from the floor above came, was disappointed at what was left of the cake, and asked us if we wanted to go to the nearby Christmas market.

We made our way to the market and lost ourselves in the stalls and lights and the festive atmosphere.

'Isn't it a smasher?'

Dami bargained for a cheap Leica and took some photos for us.

One I particularly liked featured the three of us, me, Man, and Carlisle, walking with candy apples in our hands, our backs to the lens.

Later that night, when we got back to the kitchen, Dami borrowed two sets of tweezers from the girls and took out a languid white rose from the fridge.

He used the tweezers to pull off the petals and laid them on a paper towel.

Then he took pictures.

Many pictures.

Even after the rest of us went to sleep.

***

After the holiday, my father had decided to grant me some of his attention and came back to London with me.

Upon seeing the condition of my dorm room, he commented that it looked 'no better than the state prison'.

He asked me what course I had been on and decided that engineering was not a good choice for a businessman-to-be.

He insisted that I drop out and familiarise myself with the family business.

His motto had always been 'learning by doing'.

And without the chance to say goodbye, I left the UK at the age of twenty.

I had told my roommates no lies.

My family was a cola distributor – the largest one in my country.

Not a lie. Call it an 'inoperative statement'.

I followed my roommates closely on social media.

Dami often posted his photographic work – dales and valleys, apple farms, cows grazing on lowlands, and muddy waters.

Last time I checked he had gone to the Lake District to do photo shoots for a magazine.

Carlisle succeeded in her reapplication and went to Oxford to read law.

I returned to the UK in 2019.

Having familiarised myself with the family business, I decided that it was time to resume my studies.

Shortly before the Chinese New Year, I bumped into Man on a junction near Oxford Circus.

She no longer recognised me, and she held the arm of an older lady, presumably her mother.

'Happy New Year!' I greeted them loudly.

The two giggled behind me, probably thinking what an odd person I was, greeting strangers on the streets.

The pedestrian light turned, and we went in different directions.

There was a small girl holding a model train in front of Hamleys.

I remembered Dami's words about trains and stations.

What a naive boy I was!

I laughed at myself on my way back and was no longer afraid to pass the Crossbones garden.

Perhaps, sometimes, we need a good cry, but at other times, a good laugh is better.

A Lady Who Parked
a Whale Outside
My Balcony

It was a balmy spring night in London.

By the time I retreated to my room, my head was still dizzy with numbers, Excel, and client accounts.

I washed my hands and closed the window. Mrs Mortimer, my landlady who lived next door, could no longer be heard.

The air inside was stale, with some greasy tones drifting from the Italian takeout across the road. A dead fly fell to the floor as I drew the curtains.

I washed my hands again after flushing it down the washbasin.

As the night went on, I prepared my meal the usual way: a microwave, a pack of frozen pasta, and a tasteless mouth.

I sat for a while, cleaned, and sat for another while.

That was when I heard the sobbing.

So light was it that one could mistake it for birds. Except that birds rarely came to my balcony.

At first, I thought it was Mrs Mortimer.

I gathered myself and peeked.

There was a lady sitting on the railings on my balcony. Her sobbing now turned to cries.

She was dressed rather oddly; she looked like a bit player on stage in a late Victorian play.

I stood up, unsure of what to do.

Perhaps the day had exhausted me so much I was starting to see things.

I shook my head, but her cries still crept into the room.

After some moments of struggle, I decided to go out, keeping in mind the health and safety policies for tenants at Keanley House.

'Good evening.'

I made myself sound lighthearted so as not to startle her.

She did not respond; her cries were louder, and her shoulders were shuddering.

'Now, how might I help you?'

'I...I am looking for my lost heart.'

Her voice was young and coarse, saddening the atmosphere.

'I forbid such pranks, young lady. You must get off this railing at once!'

I grabbed her wrist. It was as cold as marble.

She looked up. Her eyes were sorrowful and her lips trembled. A hole as big as a grown man's fist was revealed in her chest where her heart had once been.

St Paul's dome shined through afar.

I let go of her wrist; she fell that instant.

Sometime later, a police siren woke me, my head still heavy as bars of lead.

A dream.

Was it?

I slept through the rest of the morning and woke up mid-afternoon, my mood as blue as the rain outside.

No one had bothered me yet.

Then I realised it was a bank holiday.

I got up and went out on the balcony. Sheltering my eyes with my hands from the rain, I looked around and looked down. The filthy pavement was still there but nothing human remained.

So, it was a dream, after all...

The rain departed with the daylight, and by night, I dozed off again on my sofa. Then a high-pitched noise disturbed me.

Not a siren and not quotidian...

I opened my eyes and looked up; there was a whale outside my balcony.

A whale, yes.

'You can see me, can't you?' a voice asked me.

I recognised it from the previous night and slowly turned towards her. 'What do you want?'

'I came to claim a broken heart of mine.'

I smiled, and suddenly lost my fear.

'I do not remember capturing it.'

She giggled. 'Mister, hear me out. Please.'

Next morning, I got up early and prepared myself for an outing.

A lad stopped me as I was leaving the house.

'Morning, mate. Have you seen Mrs Mortimer? Some deed issues to discuss.'

'Hmmm... ' I pulled the door close. 'She mentioned last week that she might visit her daughter in Brighton for some fresh air.'

'Well, I reckon I'll visit her next week then.'

We said goodbye to each other, and I left for the underground in a drizzle.

The train halted at Canary Wharf, and a flock of the well-suited and well-dressed business herd left in a hurry.

I joined them, sped up my feet, and almost bumped into a middle-aged gentleman at the ticket gate.

'Sorry.' He gave me a wry smile.

'Sorry about that.' I beeped my card and fled.

On my way back home, I diverted from my usual route. I brought myself in front of the Crossbones Garden, not far from the glamorous Shard, a memorial place and once a mass burial ground for the poor, the illegal, and the immoral in London.

And where she once slept.

Her story was simple if not frequently versed:

two misplaced hearts and two forbidden identities
one illegitimate child and one illness
a war, a death, and a lost heart
with an infinite time of void to fill

***

'Did you have a good look at him?' she asked eagerly as I stepped into my room.

'Yes.'

'How was he?'

'A fine lad. Established. A banker.'

She danced around. Her whale was nowhere.

'I see your friend is not here with you today.'

'You mean Giant? No, he is out to sea with Grut. You must have heard of Grut? He was a polar bear who lived in the Thames.'

'I must confess I often failed my history classes.'

I sat down with a glass of water in my hand.

'Tell me, did he look pale? Was he tired maybe? Were his glasses clean and his umbrella heavy? Did he smell nice when you bumped into him? Was he accompanied? He could, you know, meet someone during the weekend...'

She tailed off, and I felt a tinge of jealousy enough to make my heart tickle.

We sat silently.

Our conversation from last night still lingered in the room, and her wish, that she wanted to be buried with him and sleep by his side.

In his first transmigration, he fought again in the war, and she could not bring herself to find his remains in Normandy.

In his following transmigration, he did find himself a partner. They were not able to marry, but they adopted a child, sometimes lived happily and sometimes fought, and were buried together.

'I do wish that this time his heart was mine, because mine is his only,' she said softly.

And now, he was a banker with a failing heart, and she waited patiently for their reunion.

During the following days, I tailed him from work to residence and from residence back to work.

His hours were long and his duties plenty. I watched him as he hurried through doors, his feet dragging behind, betraying his fatigue.

By the time I got back, an ambulance had pulled off close to the house.

'Poor old woman; must have banged her head on the wardrobe.'

A paramedic chatted with a man, the one who had asked me about Mrs Mortimer.

'I do feel sorry for her. People don't have the slightest idea how many elders drown themselves in their baths in this country.'

I went up to them, answered some questions and asked a few, and got back to my room.

She was there, sitting on my railing, her whale parked there.

But only I could see her.

I felt a hole was forming in my chest, my blood crystallising.

'Isn't it sad? How soon death prevails among us?' she said, in a rhetorical way.

Rain dropped like a heavy curtain, and Giant, the whale, swam across wraps of cumulonimbus and left.

***

'Help me!'

I startled and woke, her face surprisingly close to mine, but her plea cold on my face.

It was dark still and raining still.

'He...he's not well. He is not well. You need to help him! Help us, please!'

'But isn't this what...you could sleep by him when he...'

'I know. I thought I wanted it, but no, I really can't. Please help him! He is in his car. He is not well. He might crash and hurt others!'

I jerked up, pulled my coat off the hook, and flew downstairs with her by my side.

'Where is he?'

'His car...not far from Crossbones...in traffic!'

I grabbed the late Mrs Mortimer's bicycle, steadied my hands and rode fast, ran some lights, maybe more...

She came with me on her whale. 'Do please save him!'

Her cries pierced my ears.

I found the man fallen on his side, his hand on his chest, and his face distorted.

His car was parked slightly off the road shoulder, its rear obtruding, and an annoyed driver passed and honked.

I jumped off the bicycle and almost threw myself to the driver's door. My fingers were numb from the rain.

'Open the door!'

I struck at the window and yelled like mad.

'Oh! Please!'

Her cries roamed above us.

'Open it up!' I shouted as if trying to shatter the window glass.

For a second, his hand moved and pressed weakly on the lock.

I almost pulled the door down, released him from his seatbelt, and lay him down on the pavement.

'Now, relax...just relax...'

I said these words to comfort him as much as to myself.

I tore his shirt open, scraping my faint memories from a First Aid class I took at work years ago.

The following day there was no rain.

Streaks of cloud floated above us and decorated the clear sky.

'Do you wonder why London has so little sunshine?' She sat on the railing and gave a faint smile. 'Perhaps because all those capable of laughter died two hundred years ago.'

'That is not true,' I responded with a smile.

'He is bound to be with her in this life.'

She lowered her head, and a sigh slipped from her mouth.

She was referring to the lady who had rushed from her car with a portable AED when my CPR failed miserably and when we were shouting, almost crying in the rain for fear of losing him.

I looked at her.

'I have decided to see the world.'

She jumped off the railing.

'And perhaps meet him in a better state in his next life.'

The hole in her chest was less visible now.

That day we talked for hours, exchanging stories, sorrows, and a sea of other things.

Now, I could believe that it was nothing but a dream if not for the gentleman's call to express his gratitude.

And I could still remember the way she bit her lip, the way she leaned on my sofa, the eagerness in her eyes when the subject of our discussions was him; I could still remember the way her head tilted when describing her previous life.

The way she sat on my railing and made me worry, even knowing there was no need to.

The way she parked her whale outside my balcony, and the glittering of her eyes when telling stories of Grut and Giant; the way she laughed, her somewhat old-fashioned conduct. Her eyes, her smile, and the hole in her chest that made me want to supplant my own heart.

I had felt lonely all my life, and nothing came close to this.

The next day I gave myself up to the police.

For on the afternoon of the day when I first met her, a quarrel between my landlady and me had escalated into something physical, and when Mrs Mortimer hurt her head, amid her cries, I did nothing but left.

Even now I still wish that perhaps on a break from her world tours, she could come and visit me in my cell, and park her whale outside my window.

Ni Una Más
(Not One More)

There are events in one's life that one cannot miss.

Birth and death certainly belong to this category, yet other milestones bear similar importance, such as your only daughter's graduation.

I stumbled down the stairs at Kansai International Airport after two flight connections and eighteen hours of sleepless inactivity.

The night air in Japan was sweet and not as arid as back home.

A few travellers had already lined up on the train platform.

I checked my train number and joined them.

A young couple were making out behind a pillar. Their bantering drifted into my ear.

My wife and I married in early 1993. We welcomed our daughter the same year.

Two years later, my wife died in an accident during a failed local drug raid. A bullet ricocheted off a bike rim and hit her in the abdomen.

She passed away the same night, a week before our daughter's third birthday.

As a doctor, nothing was more heart-breaking than being unable to save my loved one.

I vowed at my wife's death bed that I would take the utmost care of our daughter.

I had sent her to the best schools that I could afford, and later to a prestigious university in the UK, far away from the drugs and guns in Mexico and the US.

My friends had always chided me for sending her away, asking what would happen if she spoke English better than Totonac and Spanish.

'But at least that would show she had learnt well,' I always replied.

My daughter proved me right, and she secured a MEXT scholarship from the Japanese government to pursue her PhD studies in nanotechnology in Kyoto, Japan. She completed her research with flying colours, and she was graduating next week.

'Papa, for the graduation ceremony, my professor's wife, a kind lady, has offered to lend me her *kimono*. It was a family heirloom,' she told me over Skype.

I thought for a while. 'We may not be the wealthiest of families, but I will not allow my daughter to wear someone else's clothes at her graduation. Let me find you some nice attire once I get there.'

'But the kimono. I saw it when I visited them. It was such a...'

I cut her off mid-sentence. 'I have already had my suits altered, and I need to collect them now.'

The suits, which did not need any alterations, lay quietly in my luggage.

My train came precisely on time, and it had a pink Hello Kitty painted on its doors.

I went on board, found my seat, and sat down.

My daughter had suggested meeting me at the airport, but I told her, 'You must have many preparations to make, and your father is not yet so senile as to need help finding his way.'

The jetlag made me dizzy. I drank some water and dozed a little.

After merely an hour, I arrived at Kyoto Station.

I found my way among after-work crowds to the exit, and my daughter waved at me.

'Papa!'

We hugged and parted. She looked well and seemed to be taller than the last time I'd seen her.

'See, I told you I could find my way.'

We chatted on our way to my hotel. It was called A Thousand Kyoto, and had Zen-style interior and bamboos in its lobby.

I checked in, and I was glad that the room was well-equipped and a decent size.

My friend Guillermo had told me that he once went to a conference in Japan, and the hotel room was so small that after he opened his suitcase, he had no place to put his feet.

I unpacked my luggage, washed my face, and we left for dinner.

We ate in a restaurant adjacent to a theatre.

My daughter translated the menu for me, and we ordered a few seasonal dishes. While we dined, she told me some interesting episodes she had experienced living in Japan.

'Say if you visit a Kyoto family, and someone comments that you have a nice watch, can you guess what they are trying to say?'

'That you are showing off?'

She smiled. 'They mean it's time for you to leave. And if you meet someone on the street and you chat for a while, when the other person says that you look lovely today, they mean that you better shut up and go.'

She moved on to tell me our plans for sightseeing in Japan after her graduation.

'I have booked two rooms in a guest house in Izu. They have acclaimed hot springs there.' She sighed. 'I went there with a friend during the New Year holiday, but we were denied entry to the public bath because of our tattoos. Anyways, we have two rooms this time, each with their own private baths... ' she trailed off.

We finished dinner, bought a few snacks at a convenience store, and passed a cosmetics counter that was already closed.

'We must buy Aunt Alyss some of these!' my daughter exclaimed. 'This shop is from Yojiya. They have the finest facial oil blotting paper. She would love it.'

'Perhaps we can do a little shopping tomorrow? Where do people go shopping in Kyoto?' I asked.

'Mostly around the train station so people can shop after work easily.'

She thought for a while. 'We could go to Shinkyogoku; it's a shopping district that is nice to walk around. They have many funny stores; one specialises in cat stickers.'

'Department stores would do.' I reminded her, 'First thing tomorrow, we need to look for a nice outfit for your graduation ceremony.'

She hesitated. 'But papa, my professor's wife...'

'Please...indulge your father for once. It's an important day. Your mother would be so proud of you. I am certain that she would want to see her girl outshine everyone else.'

'Alright,' she conceded. 'I'll meet you in the lobby tomorrow at ten, okay?'

We parted in front of the hotel. She was still staying in her university accommodation.

'Be careful on your way back.'

She shrugged. 'Japan is pretty safe. You have to watch out for people trying to take creepshots, but I've only encountered one so far.'

I went back to my room, took a shower, and settled on my bed, wishing my wife could be there when I woke up.

***

The next day, I had breakfast and waited for my daughter in the lobby.

Shortly before ten, she called saying she needed to go to her lab and that perhaps it would be better if I went and searched for her outfit on my own first.

The concierge pointed me to three department stores around the station. I decided to try my luck at the closest one.

There were more attendants than shoppers on that weekday. I ventured to the floor with ladies' formal wear and found a nice set that included a silk jacket with pearl decorations and a long black dress.

Subtle, but elegant.

There were two attendants in the store, one in her mid-twenties, another close to my age.

'*Konichiwa*.' I approached the young girl. 'Sorry, I don't speak Japanese. Do you happen to have this in large?'

She panicked. '*Keigo-san*.'

The other store attendant walked swiftly to us. 'How can I help you?' she asked in smooth English.

She had a name tag with the initials 'KN'.

I repeated my inquiry.

'Please wait here a moment. I will check for you.'

She rummaged through a folder. 'We currently do not have one in store, but we can ask our flagship store in Tokyo to send us one; it would take a day at most. You can pick it up tomorrow morning.'

'That's fine. Please order one for me.' I took out my wallet. 'How much should I pay upfront?'

'No need to pay now, but please leave your contact details here. We will send you a reminder tomorrow when the dress is ready.'

I wrote down the hotel's number.

I was just about to leave. Perhaps the jetlag still affected me, or maybe the floor was a little slippery, but I lost my balance and grabbed a railing.

The railing collapsed. All of its items scattered around.

'I am so sorry.' I managed to stand upright.

'Are you alright? Would you like to go to the clinic?' The attendant bent down to retrieve the items, revealing a section of her wrist; it was all bruised.

I stood there and finally said, 'No, no. I am so sorry. Let me help you.'

'Please do not be concerned.' She smiled. 'I can take care of this.'

I left the store, feeling lost.

My daughter joined me for lunch, and I asked her what the word 'san' meant. She said it would depend on the context, but most often it was used as a title of respect added to a person's name.

Afterwards, we walked to Gion, saw a few *geishas* posing for tourists, and watched ducklings playing in the river.

'They offered me a post-doc position,' my daughter told me while we rested under cherry blossoms, 'but I don't know if I should stay or leave.' She laughed. 'A Brexit quandary,' she continued. 'If I stayed, perhaps it might be more difficult.' She sighed. 'I met a Venezuelan researcher once; she specialises in biotech, she is married, and she said to me she is concerned that with her children growing up in Japan, they might speak English and Japanese, but not much Spanish.'

She moved on to say how inconvenient life would be if she didn't learn more Japanese.

In the end, all I could say was 'I will always support your decision'.

She thanked me with gratitude and a sense of foreignness that I could not place.

***

Next day, early morning, my sister called.

'If you thought *el Corte Inglés* was grand, you should come and see the department stores yourself,' I told her.

'How is our sweetie pie doing?' she asked. 'Pablo, I know there are topics that are difficult, even awkward, to discuss between father and daughter, but you should give more than a hint concerning her safety, especially in work environments.'

My sister had trained as a lawyer, and she was an avid supporter of the 'Ni Una Más' campaign denouncing violence against women in Latin America.

Before I left the country, she told me a story over dinner of a Japanese journalist who was raped by her superior and who was fighting a hard case.

My sister continued, 'Preventative measures are better than remedial action. Don't tell girls to be careful; tell those bastards to keep themselves in check.'

'I did more than hint at the issue,' I told her. 'She told me that all of her professors are very nice. Their eyes seem to be glued to their research.'

We ended our chat not long before the front desk called: the dress I had ordered was ready.

I got to the store. The young attendant was there, discussing something with a young man.

The man received me, confirmed my order, and gladly accepted my payment in cash.

I asked about the lady. They said she did not work this shift.

'Tax-free on floor seven,' the man told me before I left.

I showed my daughter the dress, and she liked it.

As we walked among the stores in Shinkyogoku, I noticed the windows on those buildings. Some were open, some were closed, and some were hidden.

A thousand windows, behind them a thousand arcades of happiness, and a thousand sources of sorrow.

A thousand Kyoto.

***

We got back to my hotel, and my daughter wished me goodnight.

We parted in front of the bamboos; she was happy.

'And Papa, after the ceremony, we are going to Uji to spend the night there.'

I watched her leave and walked to the lift while struggling with shopping bags.

A figure intercepted me.

It was the lady from the formal wear store.

'I am very sorry to bother you at this late time,' she apologised. 'We tried to contact you, but they said you were not in your room.'

'I went out with my daughter. Was anything wrong?'

She sighed defeatedly. 'We had given you the wrong size; it was not a large; it was a medium.'

I cursed myself for not checking it beforehand.

'What we can do,' her accent seeped in, 'our store in Osaka has a large size. I talked with their manager, and I will go and get it now.'

I looked at my watch; it was a quarter to ten. 'I don't want you to go to all that trouble. I should have asked my daughter to try it on today, but I am sure it will fit.'

My voice sounded less sure.

'No, no, no. It was our mistake,' she countered. 'Please don't worry; I will give the dress to the front desk, and you can return the other one when you have time,' she said determinedly. 'I will drive; it will be quick.'

I thought for a moment and said, 'If you insist, then let me go with you.'

'It is not necessary.'

'Please, I share at least half the responsibility for this.' I paused. 'I can drive right-hand cars as well.'

She thought better of convincing me and helped me to store my bags at the concierge.

We went to the parking area. She had a white van, with her company's blue copperplate logo on the door.

I got into the passenger side and watched her as she put on her seatbelt and adjusted the GPS.

'Sorry, I am a paper driver,' she said after manoeuvring the truck out of its parking spot with some difficulty.

'What's that?'

'I have my licence but have never really driven,' she explained as we joined an expressway.

I looked at her hands on the steering wheel. Her wrists were encased in white plaster.

I asked her about the injury.

She told me she fell when counting inventory, and how she had lost her balance, just like what happened to me yesterday.

A collection of bruises under white plaster.

A blatant white lie.

I told her I was a medical doctor. But I omitted how easily doctors could tell if a bruise was the result of repetitive beatings or accidental fallings.

We sat in silence for a long time.

Suddenly, it started to rain, and she turned on the windscreen wipers and the radio.

A Spanish song was playing. Its lyrics repeated the words 'cachito mió' – my little one.

I hesitated before asking if she had any children.

She told me her son had just returned from Vienna and performed in an orchestra in Yokohama.

She asked me if I was enjoying Kyoto. I told her yes and said to her that it was amazing to see such an ancient city of cultural heritage giving birth to Nintendo.

She told me that Nintendo first started as a shop that produced playing cards. And she commented that Kyoto was a place where highbrow culture meets lowbrow pursuits.

I also said that I was not used to the notion of having graduation ceremonies in spring.

She said that this way, the Japanese could celebrate cherry blossoms and their major life events together.

One song ended; another began.

She told me it was by her favourite singer. He used to work as a long-haul truck driver so he could listen to music while working.

We kept our conversations light, and in no time, we arrived at Osaka.

Perhaps some things were better left unspoken.

****

I watched her talking, bowing, and bowing again to the night security guard at the store in Osaka.

The rain had delayed us. It was around midnight when we headed back.

I offered to drive, but she would not allow it.

She told me that she had studied fashion design in college, and had spent a year in Paris.

Her husband did not want her to work when their son was little. Now, she found solace in her day job.

We drove on, this time without the radio.

Sometime after half-past twelve, her phone rang.

She pulled over and implored me to say nothing.

The call connected, and I did not need to know Japanese to understand it.

She patiently explained, but soon the man's shouting resonated in our carriage.

It continued for ten minutes, accentuated by the sounds of objects breaking.

At one point, I desperately wanted to grab her phone and tell the man at the other end to go to hell.

But her eyes told me not to.

Once the call disconnected, I turned in my seat.

'Please, you cannot carry on like this.'

She put her phone away, lips sealed.

'Have you tried legal assistance? Talk to the police? Even...' I trailed off.

My sister once had a legal aid client. Her husband was such a bastard that in the end, my sister had to seek help from a few able bodies who had worked for 'El Mencho' to discipline him for good.

'I told him that I would be home at twelve. He was only upset because I didn't get back on time.'

'You need to stop blaming yourself and trying to rationalise his actions!' I almost shouted.

'Who are you to tell me what to do?' she snapped. 'It will bring shame to both of our families. What would our son think of us? What would others think of us? My son, he... he will never marry well. As long as I keep my mouth shut, everyone is happy!'

'But what about you?' I punched my fist on my seat, trying to knock some sense into her. 'You cannot continue like this! You could die!'

'We all die eventually,' she said, composed like a philosopher. 'I do not need chivalry to come to my rescue.

Life is already too complicated for that.'

We did not speak for the rest of the journey.

***

'Thank you, *Keiko-san*. Please take care,' I said as I retrieved the wrong-sized outfit and handed it to her.

I watched her tail lights turned a corner, and she was gone.

Rain dropped incessantly.

I collected my bags and retreated to my room.

The TV turned on automatically as I collapsed on my bed.

On it played a movie, *Lost in Translation*.

Twenty-six years ago, I could not save my wife from death. Twenty-six years later, I could not dissuade another woman from slipping into gradual demise.

I asked myself what was wrong with me? Or the world?

The movie played on.

That night, I tossed like a piece of *yakitori*.

Next morning, my daughter came, oblivious to my evening escapade and my nearly catatonic state.

She looked radiant in her new attire.

I put on my suit and a smile and told myself that I would not ruin her day.

We arrived at the event early. There were happy faces everywhere.

We sat through a few speeches, and finally, my daughter went up on the stage, and she held her diploma like a trophy.

As we walked out of the hall, cherry blossom petals danced by the fountain.

'Your mother would be so proud of your achievements.' I patted her head. 'She was on her way to becoming the first female PhD from her *poblado*. Thank you for continuing her aspirations.'

I stopped, and her eyelids lowered.

We were lost in our thoughts.

A crowd had gathered near the fountain. My daughter held my arm. 'I see my professor over there. Please come, Papa.'

We walked towards the crowd.

She called out something in Japanese. A debonair gentleman turned to us.

A similarly elegant woman in *kimono* accompanied him.

'Let me introduce you. This is Professor Nakamura, and this is the *okusan*, his wife,' my daughter gestured.

'Ah. Nice to meet you, Dr Ramirez.' The professor smiled. 'Please forgive my wife for being in such a dishevelled state. She had a most terrible accident yesterday.'

The professor's wife looked at me; one of her eyes was covered with a medical patch, the other was crystal with sadness.

I reached out my hand, my voice trembling. 'Mrs Nakamura...'

Words failed me.